PUSS AND POTS

BEYOND THE ARISTOCRACY

LINDA RAE SANDE

ABOUT PUSS
AND POTS

An English potter in search of a new life, Emma Louise Avalon has left the pottery factories of Stoke-on-Trent to start her own workshop in a mining town on the Fever River in America. The red clay in Illinois will be ideal for ceramic production, and her inheritance will allow her to live comfortably.

Over the past decade, Robert Montgomery and his cat, General, have paid witness to Galena's growth due to its lead mining industry. He owns the only dry goods store in the burgeoning town, so he's sure he has everything he needs.

Or does he?

Robert's life is upended when General takes a liking to Emma. Even though she has convinced Robert to sell her pottery on commission, General's mischief-making results in an accident that forces the two to consider far more than a business deal together.

Life on the Fever River is about to heat up for these two wayward souls.

**ALSO BY
LINDA RAE SANDE**

The Daughters of the Aristocracy

The Kiss of a Viscount

The Grace of a Duke

The Seduction of an Earl

The Sons of the Aristocracy

Tuesday Nights

The Widowed Countess

My Fair Groom

The Sisters of the Aristocracy

The Story of a Baron

The Passion of a Marquess

The Desire of a Lady

The Brothers of the Aristocracy

The Love of a Rake

The Caress of a Commander

The Epiphany of an Explorer

The Widows of the Aristocracy

The Gossip of an Earl

The Enigma of a Widow

The Secrets of a Viscount

The Widowers of the Aristocracy

The Dream of a Duchess

The Vision of a Viscountess

The Conundrum of a Clerk

The Charity of a Viscount

The Cousins of the Aristocracy

The Promise of a Gentleman

The Pride of a Gentleman

The Holidays of the Aristocracy

The Christmas of a Countess

The Knot of a Knight

The Holiday of a Marquess

The Snow Angel of a Duke

The Heirs of the Aristocracy

The Angel of an Astronomer

The Puzzle of a Bastard

The Choice of a Cavalier

The Bargain of a Baroness

The Jewel of an Earl's Heir

The Vixen of a Viscount

The Honor of an Heir

The Rose of a Sultan's Son

The Ladies of the Aristocracy

The Lady of a Grump

The Lady of a Sultan

The Wager of a Wallflower

Beyond the Aristocracy

The Pleasure of a Pirate

The Making of a Mistress

The Bride of a Baronet

The Caton of a Captain

Stella of Akrotiri

Origins

Deminon

Diana

The Lyon's Den (Dragonblade Publishing)

The Courage of a Lyon

The Lady of a Lyon

Note: Translations of select titles are available in German, Italian, Spanish and Portuguese.

CHAPTER 1
AN INTRODUCTION
AND A CAT

*S*pring *1843, Montgomery Dry Goods and Mercantile, Galena, Illinois*

The faint tinkle of the door's bell signaled another arrival to his store, but Robert Montgomery was standing several rungs up on a wooden ladder, his attention on a row of ugly ceramic pots. His cat, General, was attempting to settle his large orange body into the same space as the pots, which had one of them moving close to the edge.

Too close.

The redware pottery teetered and

threatened to fall before Robert could capture and push it back into place.

"You're a pain in the arse, you know that?" he said in his slight Irish brogue, his comment louder than he intended.

"I hardly know how that could be," a feminine voice said from somewhere to his right.

Robert gave a start and nearly lost his footing on the thin ladder rung on which he was precariously perched, his gaze darting to a woman who stood near the door. He couldn't help but stare, and not because the blonde sported a small hat festooned with silk flowers and pinned at a jaunty angle, but rather because she wore a sprigged muslin gown in apple green. The fabric was unlike anything he carried in his store. For a moment, he feared a competitor had set up shop without his knowledge. Either that, or the woman was new to town.

Once he climbed down the ladder, Robert realized the style of the gown was unlike what most women in

Galena, Illinois wore. The fitted bodice ended at the waist, as did the matching spencer, and the skirt featured the silhouette of a bell, the shape probably due to the support of a half-dozen petticoats.

Below the skirt was General, for the cat had obviously jumped down from the high shelf and was about to disappear beneath the skirt's hem.

His attention lifted to her face, and he swallowed. "I... I didn't mean you, miss," he stammered. "I meant General," he added as he pointed down and discovered the cat had completely disappeared.

She bent slightly and glanced down, one eyebrow arching as if he might have told a fib. She straightened. "Did you name him that because he's the one in charge?" she asked, the hint of a teasing grin appearing at the corners of her pink lips.

Robert rolled his dark blue eyes. "Probably," he replied, attempting to ignore the heat that crept up his neck.

Now that he had a chance to see his latest customer up close, he found he didn't care where General was or what he might be doing.

If asked, he would have admitted to envy, though.

The fair-skinned woman, obviously not fresh from the schoolroom but still younger than most matrons, stood ramrod straight, her shoulders pulled back to display a pleasing figure. Besides the thought that there wasn't a dressmaker in Galena capable of such craftsmanship when it came to making the gown, Robert was also imagining what was under the muslin.

The heat on his neck moved to his cheeks, and for once he wished he had avoided shaving this morning. Besides the slight nick at the edge of his square jaw, his skin had been left feeling raw and abraded. The drop of cologne he had used stung so bad, his eyes had watered.

"I cannot decide if you are fascinated by my bosom or with my gown."

The woman angled her head to one side.

Robert jerked out of his reverie, and not only because of her comment. The way in which she said the words was unusual, her accent making her sound as if she was highborn. She also didn't sound as if she was scolding him, which he expected.

He had been staring at her bosom, after all.

"Your gown, miss. You obviously didn't have it made around here."

"I did not," she acknowledged. "Pray tell, what gave it away?"

Inhaling to answer, Robert's gaze darted to the floor again, his brows furrowing when he realized General hadn't come out from under her gown. "Uh... the fabric. I've never seen it before. I'm the only one who carries any decent cloth here in town, and I've never seen yours. I take it you're not from around here?"

He knew she wasn't. If she was, she would have been one of his customers, if for no other reason than there weren't many stores in town. He made sure to carry some goods the general store at the other end of Main didn't, products that appealed to the women in town. If they shopped for fabrics, thread, and fripperies, chances were they would buy their flour, sugar, and salt from him, too.

"Is anyone?" she countered, her blonde brow once again arching.

He cleared his throat. "Only a few of us, I suppose." From her widened eyes, Robert realized she had expected a different answer. "My father moved here from Ireland and was the original owner of this store." Although he'd had the opportunity to be a miner in his earlier years, Robert had bristled at the thought of having to answer to someone else. Inheriting a dry goods store allowed him to be his own boss.

Her gaze darting about the store, the blonde's attention settled on the redware pottery he had been arranging on the upper shelf. "As you have surmised, I am not from around here. And I am in search of a partner."

For some reason, Robert's immediate assumption was she was in search of an entirely different sort of partner than could be found in business. The thought of her in bed with him, without the green muslin gown and most of what she wore beneath, seemed like a perfect partnership.

Apparently, his cock thought so, too.

Aware of how his manhood seemed intent on escaping his breeches, Robert was relieved to remember he wore an apron covering most of his torso down to his thighs. With any luck, it was hiding the evidence of his erection.

"Partner?" he repeated, his voice cracking as if he was a nervous schoolboy. He was nearly five-and-thirty, and he couldn't recall experiencing such a reaction to any of the other women in town. Most of them were matrons, though. The younger ones tended to be married to miners or they worked in a brothel closer to the lead mines.

"I'm a potter, sir. I have set up my own workshop and kiln here in town. I am looking for someone to sell my wares."

Robert couldn't help the look of disappointment that crossed his face and caused his dark brows to furrow. "You're a potter?" he repeated. "Are you with D.A. Sackett and Co. over on Dewey?"

She stiffened. It was the second time today she had heard the name. The pottery manufacturer was still setting up their kilns. They hadn't yet produced so much as a pot, but once they did, she would have competition. "I am not." She held out a white pasteboard card. "My calling card,."

"Well now I know you're definitely not from around here," he murmured as he took the card. "I don't see many of these." He glanced at the engraved black script and arched his brow.

Avalon Pottery

Premiere pottery in the style of England's finest

Emma Avalon, Proprietress

"And yet the printer here in town did a fine job with it." She held out her right hand. Even encased in a short white glove, her fingers were obviously long and slim. "I am Miss Emma Avalon."

Robert regarded the hand a moment, trying to decide if he should shake it or kiss the back of it. He opted for the latter, which had her eyes widening. "Montgomery. Robert Mont-gomery, at your service." He nodded, almost forgetting to let go of her hand. For the brief moment he had held onto it, he confirmed she had long fingers. Knew there were no rings at the base of those fingers. Like her gown, the glove fit her hand perfectly.

Emma pulled her hand from his gentle grip and curtsied. The move-ment had her gown's hem briefly puddling onto the floorboards, and when she straightened, General's head popped out.

"General," Robert scolded. "I apologize, Miss Avalon. I wasn't aware he had…" He waved a hand as his neck heated once again. "I wasn't aware he was hiding in your skirts." He was about to say something about how lucky the beastie was, but thought better of it. "It's a rather fine skirt… dress… gown," he stammered.

"That would be because a modiste in England made it." Emma glanced down to see the cat's head once again disappearing under her hem. "Now, sir, I couldn't help but notice you already carry some pottery in your shop."

Robert blinked, his momentary jealousy of his cat quickly passing. "Uh… yes. They are rather utilitarian pieces, though." He pointed to the shelf he had been arranging upon her arrival.

"And rather crude," Emma said as she made her way to stand in front of the shelf. She turned to look at him again and huffed a breath in disgust. "I see examples of these all around town. Mostly unglazed."

"Well, there aren't exactly many potters in business around here. Once Sackett starts producing, there won't be any need."

"Oh?" She seemed surprised by his comment.

He shrugged. "Most of these pots are made by men who aren't exactly skilled. They're farmers. They make them out of necessity and sell what they can't use."

"Without a wheel, no doubt," Emma murmured, her attention still on the jugs and crocks that were lined up on the shelf.

"A wheel?"

"A pottery wheel," she replied. "I brought one with me from England. I bought a kiln in St. Louis. I've an excellent source for the red clay that can be found around here, and with lead so easy to procure, the glaze is affordable."

About to mention everyone had a source for the clay—it was plentiful near the Fever River—he realized she meant clay free from impurities, for she had pulled a small glazed redware creamer from her reticule and held it by its handle with her dainty thumb and forefinger. "A gift for you, Mr. Montgomery. Sell it if you'd like. To determine its worth."

He swallowed as he took the pottery from her, his mouth dropping open in awe when he noted how smooth and unblemished the piece seemed. A pink rose with a short stem and leaves was painted on one side. "*You* made this?"

"I did. Along with many other pieces you may wish to sell in your shop. I'm able to make crocks and jugs, pitchers and plates. Bowls. Vases. Other pieces on demand."

The bell attached to the general store's door tinkled loudly, announcing the arrival of Beatrice Sumner. The plump matron stopped short upon seeing Robert and Emma.

"Well, how do?" she said, her gaze

going to the pitcher Robert held. "Oooh. What have you there, Mr. Montgomery?"

"G'morning, Mrs. Sumner." He gave up his hold on the creamer as the matron took it into one hand and held it up to the light from the front window. "Why, Mr. Montgomery, you've been holding out on me, haven't you?"

The shopkeeper gave a start. "I assure you, Mrs. Sumner, I have not. Miss Avalon here has only a moment ago presented me with this—"

"How much?"

Robert blinked. "What?"

"How much do you want for this cream pot?" the matron asked. "I've been wantin' one for Mr. Sumner's breakfast table. Thought I'd have to send down to St. Louis for one."

Robert and Emma exchanged quick glances.

"Uh... fifteen cents?" he replied.

"Sold. You can add it to my regular order," Mrs. Sumner whipped a small sheet of paper from her reticule and held it out to him.

"Yes, ma'am," he said before giving Emma a quick look of surprise. "I'll put your order together right away. If you'd like to come back in ten or fifteen minutes, I should have it ready."

"I'll return when my prohibition meeting at the church is done," the matron said. "You're welcome to join us if you'd like." She turned to include Emma in the conversation. "It's Miss Avalon, is it not?"

"Yes," Emma replied with a nod. "It's very good to meet you."

"Just when we think we've accomplished our goal, the drunkenness in this town worsens," Beatrice complained.

Emma inhaled slowly. "Thank you for the invitation, but I've another appointment in a few minutes."

"Perhaps another time." Beatrice made her way out of the store, the bell above the door jangling with her departure.

Turning her attention back to the owner, Emma allowed a prim grin. "Will you feature my goods, Mr. Montgomery?"

Robert glanced at the door and then at the cream pot. "If this wasn't a gift, then how much would I have had to pay you for this?"

"Eight cents," Emma replied.

"And crocks?"

She shrugged. "Depends on their size. The largest would run... about sixteen or seventeen cents."

"When do I have to pay you, because most of my customers—?"

"Last day of the month for the items you sell the month prior," Emma stated.

Robert blinked. "That's fair. What about items that don't sell?"

"If you're willing to leave them on your shelf, then you needn't pay for them until after they're sold. Otherwise I can exchange them with something that might sell more quickly."

"Miss Avalon, you have a deal." He held out his right hand.

Emma grinned and shook his hand. "Thank you, sir. I'll bring by a sampling of my wares on the morrow."

Robert nodded. "I'm usually open by eight in the morning."

"Then I shall be here at eight." She curtsied, and when she straightened, she gave her skirt a quick shake.

General darted out from beneath the hem, loudly meowing his annoyance.

"I apologize." Robert frowned when he realized the cat had remained under her skirts for their entire conversation.

"Oh, you needn't, Mr. Montgomery. He's been the perfect foot warmer," she replied. "Good day, sir."

Robert watched as the potter took her leave, the bell tinkling lightly with her exit, realizing too late that she had said the word 'perfect' by holding out the first syllable for an extra count.

He glared at General. "Great. She

thinks you're *purrrrfect*," he whispered hoarsely.

Dropping to the floorboards, General stretched, yawned, collapsed onto his side, and promptly fell asleep.

CHAPTER 2
A MAN BOTHERED

A *moment later*

"Perfect," Robert murmured again, unaware he had said the word out loud.

She was, though.

Miss Emma Avalon. Blonde, with eyes the color of the aquamarine gemstones he had seen through the window of a jewelry shop in St. Louis. A voice making her sound as if she was highborn, but speaking words that were not the least bit condescending. Not like some of the other biddies who shopped in his store, always complaining they couldn't find something that would be easy to buy in St. Louis.

He supposed they couldn't help it that their husbands had elected to move to a small town with only one church and few stores. A town whose nightlife consisted of miners getting drunk at the local tavern down the street. Whatever social functions that might enliven a day here or there were due to a few industrious people—usually women—banding together to arrange a fair or a country dance. Otherwise, there wasn't much to be said for a river town his father had helped settle thirty years ago.

Whatever in the world had brought Miss Emma Avalon to such a backwater place? She had looked fresh as a daisy—probably had a few included in the flowers decorating her ridiculous hat—and behaved as if she didn't have a care in the world.

Perhaps she didn't. Perhaps being a potter was lucrative enough that she didn't have to worry about money.

Even as he considered the possibility, he realized it was unlikely she could make her living doing it. At least, not around here. If he sold every piece she brought on the morrow, he wouldn't be giving her any money until the end of the next month. What was she to do for an income until then?

"Prostitution," he murmured, which had General lifting his head from the floor. He let out a plaintive '*meow*,' as if he disagreed.

"Let's hope not." He turned to the shelf of pots and crocks. Miss Avalon was right. They were crude.

Although he didn't know anything about creating pottery, he was fairly sure it was a messy affair. The clay around Galena was red and sticky, sometimes coating the bottom of his shoes.

Did Miss Avalon handle it with her bare hands?

He tried to imagine her long fingers forming the clay into different shapes. She must have had to wet the stuff somehow to make it more malleable and stroke it repeatedly to smooth out the surface.

An image flashed before his mind's eye of her stroking his skin with her fingers. Of her hands smoothing down his chest, over his stomach, and down through the dark hair surrounding his manhood. Of one of those hands gripping it, rubbing it until it was hard and ready for a release he hadn't experienced in...

Robert blinked and dropped his head back, a soft curse sounding when he realized how uncomfortable his nether region had become with his carnal thoughts.

The sound of crinkling paper brought him back to reality. Mrs. Sumner's list. He still held the parchment gripped between a thumb and forefinger.

He mumbled something about wasting time and went about the store pulling items from the shelf and placing them on the counter, much as he did for any of his regular customers. Stepping behind the counter, he paused as he reached for a bag of flour.

Miss Avalon wasn't a customer.

When had she moved to town?

Or had she?

He shook his head. She had said she would be returning at eight o'clock in the morning, which meant she had to live nearby. There had undoubtedly been gossip about her, given Mrs. Sumner's comment. Gossip he missed because he hadn't been to church the past two Sundays.

Once again cursing softly when he realized he was woolgathering, he stared at Mrs. Sumner's list. Where his thumb had gripped the edge, the words were smudged. He glanced out the front window and then remembered the matron had said she was heading to the church for a meeting. Perhaps he could catch up to her.

He hurried out of the store and down to the end of the boardwalk and its intersection with Hill Street.

Stopping short upon seeing Mrs. Sumner, he was about to call out when he realized she wasn't alone.

Miss Emma Avalon stood with her. They were obviously discussing something of interest, given how their heads nearly touched. No doubt planning something. Plotting a scheme. Arranging to cut out the middle man when it came to Avalon Pottery.

Robert cursed.

Was Mrs. Sumner placing an order for pottery directly with Miss Avalon? After the potter had assured him Montgomery Dry Goods and Mercantile would be the exclusive source for her wares?

Whatever pleasant thoughts he might have entertained only moments ago about the gorgeous Miss Avalon fled, and Robert Montgomery squared his broad shoulders for a confrontation he knew would not end well.

CHAPTER 3
A POTTER CREATES

few minutes earlier

Emma rushed down the boardwalk fronting the various shops along Main Street until she reached the intersection at Hill Street. There to the right, not ten yards away, stood Beatrice Sumner, a huge grin brightening her round face when she spotted Emma.

"Did I do it right?" she asked with excitement, her gloved hands balled into fists.

Emma rushed up to the older matron and nodded. "You were brilliant." She took one of the woman's hands in her own. "Absolutely perfect. I feared you were going to *faint* when he said fifteen cents, though."

"Only because I feared he was going to say twenty cents," Beatrice argued. "Fifteen cents is reasonable for such a beautiful cream pot, I should think."

"I'll give you a sugar pot to go with it." Emma grinned. "For your trouble, and for your excellent acting skills."

Beatrice gave a start. "But... but I wasn't acting," she insisted. "Your pottery *is* beautiful. I shall be sure to tell all of my friends."

Emma inhaled softly, relieved to hear the older woman's assessment. Although her skills as a potter were known to those at the factory in which she worked back in England, she had no idea how her work would be received here.

Once her betrothed was out of her life, Emma had decided to follow in her late aunt's footsteps, at least when it came to living the life of a wealthy spinster. *Do what you like. Travel. Create.*

Learn, Aunt Adeline had said the year before she died.

Emma took the instructions to heart, using traditional techniques to create unique and stunning designs in earthenware. Some might have thought her a quiet and reserved person, but her passion for pottery was evident in everything she did.

"Be sure to mention they can buy it from Mr. Montgomery," Emma urged, anxious the older woman understand she would not be selling her wares directly. She didn't want any competitors angry with her, and she was certain when a middleman received a cut of the deal, her success would be more assured.

Besides, given her plan to create pottery in the mornings and paint and glaze in the afternoons, she didn't want any of the locals coming to her home. She hadn't yet arranged for a gardener to see to the overgrown landscaping surrounding her brick Italianate house.

Was there such a thing as a gardener in this part of Illinois?

"I will tell them. In fact, I really am headed to the church for our weekly prohibition meeting." Beatrice waved toward the church on the corner.

"Then I shall not keep you a moment longer." Emma curtsied. "Thank you again for your help."

Beatrice gave her a wink. "You're welcome, Miss Avalon. Good day." She hurried off in the direction of the First Presbyterian church.

Emma waited and watched the woman make her way up the hill, the incessant sounds of pounding hammers and buzzing saws a reminder of all the homes being built on Bench Street.

Bits of her meeting with Robert Montgomery flashed before her mind's eye.

Upon hearing his first words, she had detected a hint of an Irish brogue in his voice, a manner of speech he had no doubt picked up from his Irish father.

That would explain his dark, nearly black hair and those sapphire blue eyes.

"Black Irish Average height, well-built, sturdy," she murmured, barely aware she said the words out loud. "Although he did display a hint of grace when he descended the ladder." She rolled her eyes when she realized she was talking to herself, but she didn't wish to stop thinking of Mr. Montgomery and his rugged appearance.

Apparently men in this country had no qualms about showing their forearms, for the shopkeeper's white sleeves had been rolled up to past his elbows. The shirt had done nothing to hide the width of his shoulders or the breadth of his chest or the circumference of his upper arms. Upon her first sight of him, she had noticed how his muscles bulged beneath the white cotton shirt he wore, as if they were attempting to escape.

He could probably lift her with one arm. Lift her up against a wall while he had his way with her.

He would no doubt be better at it than Stephen had been. She shuddered at the reminder of her betrothed and felt relief she would never see him again. Never would she feel guilt for barely mourning his passing due to cholera.

Good riddance, she thought. Stephen had been her father's single mistake. He thought a fellow potter was good enough for his daughter and would treat her with respect and value her for her skills in the workshop.

But Stephen had no regard for anyone but himself, the selfish bastard.

Robert Montgomery seemed the exact opposite.

A shiver ran down her spine at the thought of him stripping her bare.

She couldn't recall a man in England having such a physique. "Probably from lifting heavy crates. And you're talking to yourself again." She rolled her eyes.

One of the side effects of living alone, she supposed. Except she'd been doing far more of it of late, as if there was an invisible version of herself walking alongside her, working next to her in the workshop, and standing beside her when she regarded her reflection in the cheval mirror in the corner of her small bedchamber.

That particular piece of furniture had been one of the few possessions she had brought with her from England. The oval mirror mounted on carved wooden supports had been her mother's, a gift from her father when he had achieved success as one of the most sought after potters in all of Stoke-on-Trent.

Edward Avalon had been a master at creating beautiful stoneware. An expert at shaping clay on a potters' wheel. A scientist when it came to firing the earthenware. An artist with the tiny brushes needed to create idyllic country scenes on the sides of pots and the petals of English roses on vases.

Everything Emma knew about pottery she had learned from her

father. Everything she owned in this world was because of what he had created.

Well, and because of Aunt Adeline. She had seen to it that Emma inherited what she hadn't spent on her worldly travels and extensive wardrobe.

Most of what Emma possessed in the way of clothes had been her Aunt Adeline's, much of it made in Paris or by an authentically French modiste in London. The fashionable ladies of Galena—not that there were many—hadn't yet invited her into their parlors. She supposed it would be a week or two more before she could expect an invitation. Once the biddies realized she wasn't after their husbands, they would surely welcome her.

The very last thing she wanted in this world was another controlling man thinking he could dictate what she would do in her life.

An image of Robert Montgomery once again flashed before her mind's eye, and the oddest sensation rushed down her spine. Flutterbies danced about in her stomach, and frissons of pleasure skittered beneath her skin.

Inhaling sharply, Emma turned to head home and nearly collided with Robert Montgomery.

Had she conjured him into existence with her thoughts?

"Oh, pardon me, Mr. Montgomery." She stepped back and curtsied.

The expression on the man's face was by no means pleasant, however. In fact, the shop owner looked as if he had worked himself into some sort of rage, his face red and his fists on his hips.

"Whatever is wrong, Mr. Montgomery?" Emma asked, her eyes widening in fright.

He lifted one of his hands and pointed to the departing back of Mrs. Sumner. "You don't think I know what you've done?"

Emma blinked and glanced back. The older matron had already reached the end of the block, so she was out of earshot. "Thanked Mrs. Sumner for buying the cream-pot?" she replied, all innocence. "Told her she could acquire more from you in the future?"

Robert's fierce expression softened. "Uh..." He swallowed and briefly closed his eyes. "Forgive me. I thought I was witnessing something entirely different."

Emma scoffed. "Did you think I was attempting to undercut you, Mr. Montgomery? After I made a bargain with you to be the exclusive vendor for my wares?" She made sure to sound as offended as possible. "We shook hands, Mr. Montgomery. I thought that's what passed for a contract here, but apparently—"

"It does, it does." He held out his hands in front of him, as if to ward off a blow. "But I think it's only fair to inform you that until I sell the pottery which I already have on my shelves, I really don't have room for more than one or two of your pieces."

Inhaling softly, Emma couldn't help but take another step back from the shop owner, his words acting as a blow to her midsection. The excitement she had felt only moments ago at having lined up a place to sell her pottery quickly abated.

If he hadn't seen her with Mrs. Sumner, would he still have made the comment?

"I understand, sir. Shelf space is at a premium. Perhaps I could... I could purchase the pots you have on your shelves now? To free up the space?" Her face brightened. She could certainly afford it. The utilitarian pieces might be unattractive, but that didn't mean she couldn't find a use for them in her workshop.

Robert's face screwed up in disbelief. "Are you daft?"

Emma blinked, her momentary glee quickly subsiding. "I assure you, Mr. Montgomery, I am not. The move benefits us both. You get the sale. My pottery has a shelf on which to be displayed."

It was Robert's turn to blink. He

couldn't argue with her logic. "That seems fair."

"It's settled then. I shall come back to your shop right now and buy those pots from you." About to walk the few steps back to Main Street and to his store, she paused when she noted his attention had once again gone to the next street up the hill. "What is it?" Her brows furrowed. "What had you leaving your shop in the middle of the day?"

Robert gave a start, his attention once again darting to the end of the block. He held out a sheet of paper. "Mrs. Sumner's list," he said. "The writing is smudged, and I can't make out a couple of the items on it." He grimaced.

"Let's see if I might be able to decipher it." She took the scrap of parchment from him.

"Decipher it?" he repeated, a hint of humor replacing his momentary worry. "You make it sound as if it's in some sort of code."

"Well, most lists are," Emma replied, her attention on the printing. "At least Mrs. Sumner has excellent penmanship."

Most of the grocery list was legible —beans, lentils, and dried peas—until where a gloved thumb had smeared the charcoal. Above it was an amount of flour, and below was an amount of salt. "Five pounds of sugar," she announced. She handed him back the paper.

Robert frowned as he studied the writing. "How can you be sure?"

"It's most definitely sugar, sir. I admit I am not positive as to the number of pounds, but given the amount of flour and salt she's asking for, five pounds is a logical assumption.Besides, Mrs. Sumner seems to be a reasonable woman. I'm sure she'll understand if you make sure to include her list in the box with her order. Then she'll see for herself what you were working from."

Although Robert had never heard the words 'logical assumption' spoken by a woman before, he decided he had to agree with Emma. "Very well." His darted his eyes to the side. "Were you serious about buying the pottery?"

"Yes, let me take care of that now," she said as he turned and paused until she was walking alongside him.

"They'll be too heavy for you to carry," he warned. He opened the door and held it for her.

The tinkling of the bell was accompanied by·a loud *crash*, and Emma inhaled sharply as shards of broken crockery scattered across the floor. She quickly stepped out of the way as Robert rushed into the store.

"Careful," Emma said, a gloved hand going to her mouth.

A loud '*meow*' sounded from the shelf of pottery.

Her attention, as well as Robert's, shot to General, who was in the process of shoving another pot to the edge of the shelf.

Before Robert could say or do

anything, the crock teetered and fell over the edge.

"General!" Robert yelled. He attempted to capture the cat, but a responding '*meow*' was followed by an orange blur as General jumped down and fled from the scene.

Emma tiptoed her way through the shards, her gaze once again returning to the pottery shelf to see that only one crock—a rather large one—still remained. "I suppose I'll be buying just the one." She spread open the edges of her reticule and pulled out her coin purse. She turned to discover Robert staring at her as if *she* had been the one to knock the pots from the shelf. "Have you a broom, sir? And a waste bin of some sort? I can see to sweeping up while you fetch the crock."

Shutting the door a bit harder than he intended—the tiny bell jangled furiously before settling into a pleasant tinkle—Robert pulled a broom from behind the adjacent counter and handed it to her.

He raised an eyebrow. "I don't suppose you have any use for broken crockery?"

Emma understood the anger tingeing his voice. From her visit earlier, she had counted six items on the shelf. Now there was only the one crock. If she'd had a cat who destroyed five pieces of pottery, she, too, would be furious. "I know it doesn't seem like it now, but there's a German proverb that says breaking an object of glass or porcelain predicts good luck in one's life." She began to sweep.

Robert scoffed as he took the three steps up the ladder and hoisted the crock from its perch. He was careful in his descent before placing the pottery on the counter.

Watching from where she swept, Emma had to suppress her gasp at seeing how his muscles bulged across his back and upper arms as he hefted the heavy pot.

"If that's the case, I'm due a good deal of good luck, wouldn't you say?"

"Indeed, Mr. Montgomery." She gathered her sweepings into a pile. "Might I suggest you keep these larger potsherds?"

"Whatever for?" He returned his attention to Mrs. Sumner's list. In all the excitement, another line of print had been smudged.

"You can use it for mulch, sir. In your garden."

"Don't have one of those, but... I suppose I have a customer or two who might be interested."

She handed the broom to him. "How much do I owe you for the crock?"

"Twenty-five cents," he replied.

Suppressing the urge to argue, Emma pulled a coin from her purse and gave it to him. "Thank you, Mr Montgomery. I'll return in the morning with a variety of pottery for your shelf, and if I might make a suggestion?"

He looked at her, suspicious. "Only if you can decipher this newly smudged line," he countered, holding up Mrs. Sumner's list.

"Ten pounds of flour and five pounds of sugar," she stated. "Perhaps the pottery should go on a lower shelf, where it will be easier for your customers to see and easier for you to retrieve?"

Robert glanced up at the shelf, immediately understanding her reasoning. "Perhaps," he replied. "Which means I need to do a bit of rearranging."

"The winter clothing can go higher now that spring is upon us," she suggested.

He gave her a quelling glance. "Good day, Miss Avalon."

"Good day, Mr. Montgomery."

Emma lifted the heavy crock into the crook of one arm, curtsied, and made her way out of the dry goods store and down Main Street.

*A*lthough Robert knew he should continue gathering Mrs. Sumner's order—she would be returning from her meeting within the hour—he didn't immediately resume the work. Instead, he swept the smaller potsherds into a dustpan. Deciding he could dump them into the cheroot snuffer outside his door, he did so. Before going back into the store, he paused and watched the departing figure of Miss Emma Avalon as she made her way west, the sway of her bell skirt hypnotizing him.

"I could use a little luck," he whispered.

CHAPTER 4
A BARGAIN IS
STRUCK

*T*wenty *minutes later*

Her arms shaking from having carried the heavy two-gallon-sized crock from Mr. Montgomery's store to her brick home nearly a half-mile away, Emma lowered it to the floor of her workshop and winced. In the light from the west windows, the crude piece appeared even worse than it had in the shop.

"Refuse bin," she said to herself as she moved it next to the maple desk she had acquired in St. Louis. The last leg of her journey from Stoke-on-Trent had been on a riverboat going from the

Gateway to the West and brought her, a family of five, and a dozen miners to Galena.

Home to lead mines, two rivers, and earth filled with red clay, it was the perfect location in which to set up her workshop. If only there had been a decent building already in existence on the property she had purchased. The one currently housing her kiln and pottery supplies had obviously been assembled quickly, without much care for aesthetics or the weather in the winter.

At least the red brick house was in good order, its previous owner one of the early mining company supervisors. He hadn't even lived in the two-story Italianate-style dwelling a year before deciding to have a much larger Greek revival home built up on Bench Street.

Emma couldn't imagine how his family of ten and all their furnishings would have fit in what on the inside was a typical six-room townhouse in the middle of London.

Her meager belongings from England were scattered throughout the small house. She hadn't bothered bringing much with her other than two trunks of clothing, her best pieces of pottery, the potter's wheel, and the cheval mirror. Her other furnishings—a bed, dresser, settee, side chair, round table, a variety of caryatids, and the kiln—had arrived on the same steamboat as the desk, all ordered during her month-long stay in the burgeoning city on the Mississippi River. A burly porter had arranged for everything to be loaded onto a dray cart and pulled to the house by a pair of mules, and then he had seen to unloading it and moving it all into her house. All for only a dollar.

As for the lean-to, Mr. Cruthers, one of the construction men working on the new houses in Bench Street, had promised to build a sturdier room on the back of her current house to hold the kiln.

Suddenly aware of movement

somewhere nearby, Emma froze. "Who's there?" Her heart hammered in her chest as a small furry creature darted across the floor. "A mouse? I thought I'd gotten rid of all of you." She let out a screech when it was followed by a much larger flash of orange fur.

She clasped her hands to her chest as she backed up against her desk. "General?" she called out, remembering the cat from the dry goods store.

Whatever was he doing here?

A moment later, the large creature emerged from behind a box of red clay, looking ever so proud of himself. "*Meow*."

"You scared me half to death. But I thank you for whatever it was you just did. That is, if you caught the mouse."

General gave her what she surmised was an expression of offense before he rolled himself into a sunbeam and stretched out on the floor. She could practically feel the vibrations from his purring through the wooden floorboards.

"Yes, do make yourself comfortable," she murmured as she doffed her spencer and pulled on an apron. She expected the cat would take his leave and then wondered how he had entered the house in the first place. Glancing toward the front door, she confirmed she hadn't left it open. Had he sneaked in under her skirts?

"I don't have time to pet you. If I'm to take all my remaining finished pottery to Mr. Montgomery's store, I need to make some pieces to go into the kiln on the morrow."

General narrowed his eyes before his head dropped to the floor.

Deciding he wasn't in the way, Emma went to work.

Cutting a section of clay from a damp cloth-covered hunk, she wet her hands and began working it, kneading it and folding it over and banging it onto a slab of marble as she smoothed her wet hands over its surface.

Once it was soft enough, she tossed it onto her wheel and began to pedal.

After dipping her hands into a pot of water next to her wheel, she held the lump of clay between her cupped hands, smoothing the shape into a round cylinder. Then she poked a wet finger down the middle to create a hole and began widening the opening, lowering her hand and spreading out the base of a crock until it was the correct width.

Drawing the fingers of each hand up the inside and the outside at the same time, she extended the height of the crock until it reached the marking on the ruler she had mounted on the wheel's base. She wet her hands again and smoothed the surface until she was satisfied there were no signs of her finger marks. Before she stopped pedaling, she employed a thumb and forefinger to create an even rim at the top edge. Using a flat metal spatula, she loosened the crock from the wheel and moved it to a drying shelf.

She repeated the process and made several jugs, the sugar-pot she had promised Mrs. Sumner, and finally a vase.

With the sun about to set, there wasn't enough light to continue without a candle lamp, so she used a wet rag to wipe down the potter's wheel then cleaned her hands in the vat of water.

Emma removed her apron and was about to head to the kitchen for a cup of tea when she discovered General was exactly where he had fallen asleep, the sunbeam long since gone.

"Oh, dear. Mr. Montgomery will be wondering what's become of you." She pulled on her spencer. "Come. We need to get you home."

Although General opened his eyes and seemed intent on listening to her words, he didn't seem motivated to move.

Scoffing, Emma pulled on her gloves and gathered a few smaller items into a wooden tray with handles. A trip to Montgomery's Dry Goods and Mercantile now would save her from having to go in the morning. "Well, are you coming?" She grabbed the strings of her reticule, balancing the tray on one arm while she held the door with the other.

General darted past her and out the door. He paused, though, as if he was waiting for her.

"I'm coming." She pulled the door shut.

CHAPTER 5
A SHOPKEEPER'S
BAD LUCK

A few minutes later

Not exactly walking with her as Emma made her way back to Main Street, the cat meandered and disappeared, reappeared and raced ahead once they stepped onto the boardwalk that fronted the shops on the north side of the street.

Pushing open the door for Montgomery's Dry Goods and Mercantile, Emma heard the tinkling of the bell followed by Robert Montgomery cursing.

Loudly.

She paused, as did General.

"We're closed," he shouted from somewhere beyond a curtain near the counter.

"Mr. Montgomery? It's Emma Avalon. I've brought some pottery along with your cat. He apparently followed me home."

From the other side of the curtain, Robert appeared. He had removed the apron he had been wearing earlier and wore only a white shirt, Nankeen breeches, and black boots, and he was holding a red cloth around one hand.

Emma blinked, and she blinked again when she realized the cloth was red not because it had been dyed that color, but rather because he was bleeding. "Oh my, whatever has happened?" She set the tray on the counter, kicked the door shut, and rushed to him.

"It's nothing. I cut myself is all." He grimaced when Emma reached out to lift a corner of the cloth. He jerked his hand back. "Don't. You'll ruin your gloves."

"Cut with what?" She glanced

about in search of a chair. "Sit down." She stripped her gloves from her hands.

"Broken pottery, if you must know," he replied, obviously annoyed. He turned around and led her behind the curtain and into a small room with a fireplace, bookshelves, and an uphol-stered chair. A hurricane lamp had already been lit, as had the fire. For a moment, Emma was reminded of a modest drawing room in an English townhouse, but this one smelled of pipe tobacco, musk and wood smoke, and it was half the size.

"Oh, dear. This is all my fault." She looked about for anything to clean the wound.

"I hardly see how," he argued.

"Do sit down.

He nodded toward a pony wall at the back of the space. "There's water in the kitchen back there, if that's what you're looking for." Following her orders, he sat in the room's only chair and settled back, peeking under the cloth to discover his wound might be worse than he thought. He cursed, but made sure to do it in a whisper.

Emma hurried to the other side of the short wall and discovered a pitcher and bowl on a valet stand. A small mirror was mounted in the middle and the hooks on either side held his apron and a coat. The water in the bowl was stained red, evidence he had already attempted to clean the wound.

The water pump hooked over a deep sink, and she bent down to see that a pipe was connected to the drain and going through the floor.

"It's not exactly modern plumbing," Robert called out, curious as to what she was doing. "But it saves me from having to haul water in and out."

"That's all I need to know." She dumped the contents of the bowl into the sink and pumped fresh water into it. "Do you have any bandages?" She would sacrifice the bottom edge of a petticoat if he didn't. Helping herself to a washcloth from the valet stand, she dipped it in the bowl and wrung it out.

"I was on my way to get some. From the store," he said.

About to ask which store, Emma noted his arched brow and realized he meant his own. "Let's get this bleeding stopped first," she whispered as she approached with the wet cloth.

She knelt before him and gingerly unwrapped the soaked cloth. Hissing, she gave him a glance before pressing the washcloth to the apparent source of blood—a cut in his palm about an inch long. "A shard of pottery did this?" she asked in disbelief. "I do believe stitches are called for," she added, secretly wishing there was a physician nearby. She knew as well as he did there wasn't, though. No dentists, either. "Where do you keep your bandages? And thread?"

"Catgut is with the bandages, and if I remember right, I think there might be a needle there, too." Before she arrived, he had already decided he was going to stitch up the wound himself. "Now that you're here, you can thread the needle for me."

He gave her brief instructions as she rushed down one aisle and stopped before a roll of gauze, strips of linen, a ball of catgut, and a curved needle stabbed into a square of pasteboard. Not finding any scissors, she remembered she had a pair of embroidery scissors in her reticule and grabbed it before heading back to the parlor.

Emma unrolled a length of catgut and held it out, her gaze darting to one of the cats.

"It's not made from cat guts," Robert said, as if he could read her mind. "Probably sheep."

"Do I need to boil it or... hold it over the fire?"

"Probably, but..." He shook his head.

Emma went about threading the catgut and once again knelt before the shopkeeper.

"Let's take a look." She sucked in a breath when he held out his hand. The washcloth appeared to have stopped the bleeding, but if he so much as flexed his hand, it would begin bleeding again. "Do you have brandy? Or... or whiskey?"

Despite his dark mood, he nodded to the bookshelves on one side of the fireplace, where a bottle of brandy fronted a number of cloth-and leather-bound books. A crystal tumbler sat next to it. She pulled the cork on the bottle and poured a generous amount into the glass before taking a long draught.

"Hey!" Robert protested. "I thought that was for me."

"Oh, it is." She poured more into the glass until it was nearly full and handed it to him.

"Have you done this before?" he asked as she held his wounded hand in one of hers with the curved needle and catgut poised in the other. To provide more support, she rested the back of her hand on the arm of the chair and angled his hand so the flame from the hurricane lamp illuminated his palm.

"I have not. Have you?"

"Do you know how to sew?" he

countered in a quiet voice. He drank deeply from the glass of brandy.

She inhaled softly and then realized he probably didn't know that every English miss knew how to sew and embroider. "Of course I do." She didn't bother to hide her offense. She gingerly poked the needle into his palm near the cut and pushed it beyond the opening, angling it up until there was enough needle to capture on the other side.

"Just don't pull it all the way through," he murmured, doing his best to keep his hand still as she pulled the length of catgut until only a short tail remained showing.

"I wouldn't have thought those crude pots would have such sharp edges," she murmured as she worked, nervous because he watched her every move. Given the waning light from the room's only window, she relied on the light from the hurricane lamp to see.

"Me, neither," he replied. "Turns out, there was an arrowhead embedded in one. So much for the good luck you promised."

Emma winced at hearing the censure in his voice. "An arrowhead? Are you referring to something to do with archery?" Although she knew that daughters of well-to-do merchants and aristocrats learned how to shoot arrows with a bow, she had never done so.

He drained the glass of brandy. "The Indians make them for their arrows. From rocks."

"So... it was *in* the clay?" she asked before she paused in her task and looked up, her eyes rounding. "Or... or do you suppose it was added *after* the pot was formed?"

Robert furrowed his brows. "Probably already in the clay. Which means you'll want to be careful when you're working with the stuff."

She took the last stitch and tied it off with the tail piece. "I usually draw a knife through a hunk of clay several times before I start to work with it. To be sure there are no rocks." She cut the remaining catgut with the small scissors.

"You do good work," Robert remarked as he examined the six even stitches. "I should be able to remove them in a week or two."

"Let me wrap it for you. You'll need a reminder to not to stretch out your hand."

"Oh, I think the pain will be reminder enough, but..." He sighed. "Go ahead."

Emma wrapped a gauze strip around his hand several times and then covered it with a linen wrap, securing part of it around the base of a finger before tying off the ends. "Is that too tight?"

He shook his head. "It's fine. Thank you."

Emma gathered the leftovers. "It's the least I can do. Hopefully you don't have far to go to get home." Despite her hands being full, she easily stood and made her way back into the store.

"About fifteen steps, mostly up.

There are two rooms above the store." He pointed to a door at the end of the kitchen.

"How convenient." A frisson shot through her abdomen at the thought of his bedroom being so close. Once she had returned the bandages and gauze to the store shelf, she returned to the parlor to retrieve her spencer. "Did I guess right with Mrs. Sumner's order?"

He scoffed. "You did indeed."

"I've brought the pottery items I promised. I couldn't help but notice you emptied a lower shelf. Is that for my pottery?"

"It is."

"Then if you'd like, I'll fill it with what I brought. With any luck, General won't bother them."

Robert watched her pull on her spencer. "You said something about bringing him back?"

"He was in my workshop all after-noon," she replied, straightening her sleeves. "Chased a mouse and then made himself at home and took a nap."

Chuckling, Robert settled his head against the back of the chair. "Sounds like General. But..." He glanced down at the orange feline who watched him from next to the fireplace. "That's... not General."

About to move two of the pieces of pottery from the tray onto the empty shelf, Emma paused and stared at Robert before turning her gaze onto the cat. "Are you sure?"

He chuckled again, his amusement lighting his face and forcing crinkles to appear at the edges of his eyes. "Quite sure." His used his wrapped hand to indicate another cat sleeping next to his chair.

Emma nearly dropped the jug she was holding. "Oh, dear. They look *exactly* alike."

CHAPTER 6
A POTTER PROVIDES
BETTER LUCK

Robert stifled a chuckle. The woman looked so stunned, he was afraid she might faint at seeing not one, but two orange cats. "They should look alike," he replied. "They were litter mates."

Emma scoffed softly, her gaze darting between the two felines. "Are they both yours?"

He seemed to think on it a moment. "Do cats ever actually belong to anyone? I've always had the impression *I* was the one who belonged to *them*."

"So, is that why one is named General? Because you report to him?"

A full-throated laugh erupted from Robert, which had Emma grinning. "He is in charge," he remarked. "They both are, truth be told."

"What have you named the other?" She placed the last piece of pottery on the shelf and stepped back to admire the arrangement, barely aware the cat in question had joined her.

"Admiral."

Sure he was teasing her, Emma returned to the parlor. "You're joking." She picked up her reticule and placed the pair of dainty scissors in its case.

"I am not," he insisted. For the first time, he noticed she was gathering her things. "What are you doing?"

"Taking my leave."

"Where are you going?"

"Well, home, of course."

"It's almost dark out there," he argued. "I started a pot of tea before this happened." He held up his injured hand. "I'm sure the water is still hot. Will you join me for a cup?"

She gave a start. "After what's

happened to you on this day, I can hardly believe you want *my* company," she said in a quiet voice.

Both cats sounded plaintive '*meows*' at the same time.

Robert chuckled softly. "It's up to you, but I've certainly learned not to cross either one of them."

Emma inhaled, a frisson darting up her spine when she saw how he gazed at her. For a moment, she wondered if he was drunk from the brandy. "I was about to have a cup of tea before I discovered Admiral was still in my house. So... all right, I'll stay for a cup." She glanced into the kitchen area. "I can see to it."

"I should lock the door," he said. "It's well past closing time, and the miners have already come into town for the night. I'd rather not have any of them thinking they can shop this late in the day. After they've had too much to drink, they tend to think they can help themselves."

"I can see to that, but you'll have to

let me out when I leave later." As she bolted the shop's door, her gaze went beyond the front window. The sun had already set, and Main Street appeared to have taken on an orange-red tinge.

She stepped back when a group of men made their way toward the tavern. Even if she left now, it would be twilight or completely dark before she reached her house, and the moon wouldn't be up for hours.

Her heart raced as she considered her options—beg for hospitality or hope she didn't cross any drunken miners on her way home. She remembered Beatrice's efforts to force prohibition on the small town, and now she understood the woman's concerns.

She headed to the kitchen, closing the curtain separating the store from the parlor, and found a pair of teacups and saucers. "Is there a place for me to sit?" She poured hot water over a tea strainer.

"We'll go upstairs," he answered, his voice close.

Emma turned around to discover he was directly behind her. He might have come closer, but his legs would have disturbed her skirts. "Do you have biscuits?" she asked in a whisper.

His brows furrowed. "I have the stuff to make them, of course," he replied before a grin appeared. "Oh, you mean cookies, don't you?"

She nodded. "I'd quite forgotten the other word for them."

Reaching over and around her with his good hand, he pulled a tin from a shelf. "Mrs. Cruthers brought me some a few days ago." With one arm, he held the tin against his chest while he pulled the lid off with his good hand.

"That was very kind of her." She finished pouring the tea.

"You might not say that once you taste them," he countered, before he bit into one. The resulting crunch was loud.

Emma had trouble suppressing a laugh. "Mr. Montgomery—"

"Call me Robert." He captured a

crumb at the edge of his lips with his tongue.

She inhaled softly. "You're incorrigible."

"My mother used to say that to my father." He arched a dark brow. "When you say it, it doesn't make me sound so bad, though."

Her eyes rounded. "Whatever do you mean?"

"Your accent. The way you say words, all proper like, but not snooty. You could call me a bastard and I wouldn't mind."

"I would never call you that, Robert," she countered.

"You might after what I'm about to do to you." His warning was barely audible.

Emma inhaled, her eyes rounding when he bent down and touched his lips to hers. She didn't back away, though—not that she could since she was pressed against the front of the sink—and instead parted her lips in invitation.

Before she knew it, his lips captured hers. She gripped the fabric of his sleeves with both hands in an effort to stay upright.

She tasted the cookie he had just eaten, determining he had indeed been teasing about their flavor. Her knees felt as if they had turned to jelly, if not from how close he stood, then because of the brandy she had drunk far too quickly before she had stitched his wound.

She let out a mewl of protest when he pulled away. He grinned. "I think one of us might be feeling a bit drunk," he whispered.

"Oh," she replied, disappointment evident in her response. "Does that mean you wouldn't have kissed me if you were sober?"

"*I'm* not the one who's feeling the brandy," he countered, his brow once again arching as a grin youthened his face.

"It was excellent brandy," she whispered, a moment before she stood on tiptoes and kissed him. Her hands reached up to his shoulders as she pressed against him. She moaned when his tongue invaded her mouth and slid across her teeth.

Stephen had never kissed her like this. He had only touched his lips to hers, and had never opened his mouth to claim her lips as Robert was. Had Stephen done so, Emma was sure she would react in revulsion. With Robert, she wanted the kiss to go on and on. Wanted him to hold her closer, and then was sure he could read her mind, for his good hand had moved to the small of her back and was pulling her hard against him.

When they pulled away, breathless, she stared up at him, her eyes finally focusing on the blue pools of his. "You must think me fast."

An expression of uncertainty crossed his face. "I have no idea what that means."

"I don't usually kiss men I hardly know."

"Well I should hope not." He swallowed around a lump in his throat.

"I don't usually kiss men at all."

"Then it seems I am a very lucky man."

Emma's eyes rounded before she gave him a brilliant smile. "I am so pleased you think so. It means the proverb about breaking glass is true."

He angled his head to one side, not about to argue with her. Holding her like this—her shoulders wrapped in his arms and their bodies pressed close—did have him feeling as if his luck had changed. Had him wishing they had met long ago instead of only this morning.

What sort of life might they have had if she had appeared...?

Robert gave his head a shake. He hadn't been looking for someone back then. Hadn't been of a mind to share a hardscrabble life in a town barely settled. The responsibility for the store had been quite enough in his twenties, especially after his parents' death.

He hadn't even been looking for a woman this morning, and yet Emma Avalon had waltzed into his store ready to offer him a partnership in her pottery scheme. Given how she had kissed him, perhaps she was looking for more.

In response to her comment about the proverb, he grinned. "I blame the cats."

"Credit them, don't you mean?" she countered, finding Admiral and General were watching them with great interest.

"Now you've gone and done it," he said as he lowered his forehead to hers.

"What have I done?"

"Whatever it is they want you to do."

"Which is... what?"

Robert glanced back at General and arched a brow. "Well?"

"*Meow*." General replied, as if he was providing some sort of answer.

Admiral joined General, the two posed in identical sitting positions and looking every bit the twins they were. They gazed at Robert and Emma for a moment before they settled onto their sides.

"See?" Robert said, turning to discover Emma staring at him rather than the cats. Beneath his hold, something shifted in her.

"Does that mean they will allow me to spend the night here in your shop, seeing as how it's far too dark for me to walk home?" Emma's voice was quiet.

Robert's brows drew together, his good humor gone in an instant. "Miss Avalon—"

"Emma. You can call me Emma."

"Emma, I have no intention of allowing you out of my sight for at least the next twelve hours. They won't, either."

She blinked up at him. "That long?"

"And you won't be spending it here in the store," he added.

"I won't?"

He shook his head. "There's a bed upstairs."

Her gaze darted toward the stairs. "Will you be in it?"

It was Robert's turn to blink. "If you'll allow it."

"Shouldn't I insist on it?" She glanced over at the cats, and this time Admiral responded with a rather loud, "*Meow*."

Robert scoffed softly. "How much brandy did you drink?"

"Not even half a glass. I feared I might faint, seeing as how you were bleeding so badly."

"You certainly didn't seem as if you were going to faint. You were rather bossy, in fact."

"Was I?" She swallowed. "I was nervous, is all. I haven't sewn a stitch in some time."

"Were you worried, maybe? About me?" His voice held a hint of hope.

She nodded. "Indeed. I spent the entire afternoon imagining what it would be like to make love to you, and if you had perished because of a broken..."

Unable to continue when he pressed a finger to her lips, Emma glanced up to discover his eyes had darkened until they were nearly black.

"You don't have to imagine." He reached behind her and helped himself to one of the cups of tea, draining it in a single gulp. "I am more than willing to allow you to find out first-hand."

Emma's eyes widened. She turned and helped herself to the other cup of tea, drinking it in two gulps. "You're quite sure I wouldn't be taking advantage?"

Robert blinked before he dropped his forehead to hers. "Something tells me I won't be opening the store by eight o'clock in the morning," he whispered, before leading her to the stairs.

Glancing at the two cats who watched from in front of the fireplace, Emma gave them a wink, gathered up her skirts, and hurried up the stairs.

CHAPTER 7
A PURRFECT NIGHT

A few minutes later Robert lit the only candle lamp in the bedroom and worried Emma had changed her mind when she stood at the end of his bed and sighed audibly. He had taken the time to make it that morning, but there was no counterpane—only a folded down blanket, two feather pillows, and the linens beneath. At least he had dark curtains covering the windows. "I take it you've changed your mind?"

Emma shook her head. "Oh, I haven't changed my mind. I am hoping it doesn't break, is all." She turned and reached out to undo the button at the top of his collarless shirt.

Despite the seriousness of her words, Robert couldn't help but laugh. "Good God, what are you planning to do to me?" He grinned when she pulled up on his shirt tails until they were free of his breeches. He divested himself of the garment in one quick move then sobered when he saw her look of uncertainty.

Or perhaps it was awe.

"You haven't seen a shirtless man before?"

"Only in the form of marble statues. Mostly Greek Gods." She took in the crisp curls dusting his chest. His nipples were erect, much like hers were. Despite the soft fabric of her chemise under her corset, they felt as if they were chafing.

He stepped behind her. "Have you made love before?" he asked in a whisper, undoing the row of buttons at her back and the one holding her skirt closed at the top. Beneath it, he discovered ties for her petticoats and began undoing one after the other. He was surprised there were only three.

Emma winced. "I wouldn't call it that. Not given the way he..." She stopped and took a deep breath at the same moment her skirts and petticoats dropped to the floor in a round puddle. She lowered the bodice from her arms and tossed it onto the pile. Left wearing only a corset over a chemise and her stockings, she suddenly felt vulnerable.

"Were you betrothed to him? Are you... still?" His voice cracked when he stepped in front of her and glanced down at her shapely limbs. The thin chemise ending at the top of her knees did nothing to hide the dark triangle at the apex of her thighs.

"No." She stepped out of the huge ring of fabric. "He died a few months before I left England. And do not be concerned. I did not mourn him, for he had no regard for anyone but himself," she murmured. Saying the words out loud seemed to embolden her.

"I cannot imagine a man having no regard for you." Robert undid her corset fastenings with his good hand. He paused, studying the hook and eye closures.

"What about you? Is there a...?" Her eyes suddenly rounded. "Are you betrothed? Or... or were you married?" She knew from his meager furnishings and the rooms below that no woman had ever been in his parlor. But it didn't mean there wasn't a lady in his life.

"Neither." He paused. "Am I doing this right?" he asked when he finally had one of the hooks undone at the bottom.

"I cannot imagine how you could do it wrong." Even through the stiff fabric of her corset, she felt the warmth of his hands, and the careful way he barely touched her as he struggled with the hooks.

"Besides the..." He clamped his mouth shut, about to mention the prostitutes that serviced the miners. "There aren't many unmarried women about.

And it's taken a few years to make my living." He swallowed when only the top two fastenings were left to undo.

Emma placed a hand over his good one, guiding it so it cupped one of her breasts. She easily undid the last two hooks and pulled the corset from around her middle.

Although it didn't provide enough light for the entire room, the candle lamp was close enough to illuminate her. Emma felt far too exposed, but then she saw how the light played off Robert's chest, and she inhaled softly. "You're so... broad," she whispered.

"Is that bad?" He rubbed a thumb over one of her nipples.

She inhaled sharply, which had her breast filling his hand. He repeated the move on her other nipple, and she mewled softly. "No," she managed as she placed the pads of her fingers against his warm skin, trailing them through dark curls and down his stomach to the top of his breeches. She knew what caused the bulge below that, even if she hadn't seen one directly. Cupping her hand along its length, she gently pressed it.

Robert inhaled sharply and covered her hand with his good hand. "Careful," he whispered hoarsely.

She pulled her hand away. "Did I hurt you?"

"Exactly the opposite." He fumbled with the buttons of his breeches.

Emma understood his struggle and immediately went to work undoing the fastenings. The front fall of his breeches opened, and his manhood sprang out as she pushed the garment down his hips. "Oh, my," she whispered.

"Is that a good 'oh my' or an 'oh my' of disappointment?" He sat on the edge of the bed and pulled his boots and stockings from his feet, placing the footwear at the end of the bed.

Emma gave a one-shouldered shrug. "Mayhap of fright?" She took in his nakedness from head to toe and back to his crotch when he stood.

"How old are you?" he asked in a

quiet voice, closing the distance between them in two steps.

"It's not polite to ask a woman her age." She pressed her front to his, cradling his rigid manhood against her soft belly.

"What year were you born?" He kissed her forehead.

"Eighteen-sixteen." She wrapped her arms around his chest and pressed her cheek against the front of his shoulder.

"The Year of No Summer," he whispered.

She inhaled softly and pulled away to glance up at him. "How do you know about that?"

"We experienced it here. Did it happen in England, too?"

"Oh, very much so." She resettled her cheek against his warm skin. One of his arms had wrapped behind her shoulders while the other was at the back of her waist. "At least, from what I've read about it." She glanced up at him. "You're very warm."

"There's a reason," he remarked dryly.

She pulled one of her hands from behind his back and smoothed it between them until it came in contact with his manhood. Drawing a finger down the side of it, she paused when his breathing hitched.

"It's so soft."

"I beg your pardon?"

She blinked and then drew the finger up the vein that throbbed along its length. "The skin. It's like velvet." She added her thumb and gently squeezed, her hold on him giving way when he pulled back. "Like velvet stretched over an iron rod."

"I don't think it's ever been this hard." He took her hand and guided her fingers to wrap around the shaft and then moved them up and down, his breaths shortening when she tightened her hold. "I fear if you do that much longer, I'll come too quick."

"Won't you feel pleasure then?" A bead of moisture had formed at the tip of his manhood. She drew her thumb over it, spreading it out as Robert inhaled sharply.

"Yes, but I want you to feel it, too," he managed to get out between gasps for air.

Emma glanced up at him, one brow furrowed. "So... making love can be pleasurable?"

He nodded before he realized she hadn't experienced the intense pleasure of sexual congress. "It's supposed to be."

"Will you teach me? What to do...?"

She couldn't finish the sentence when he suddenly pulled the chemise from her body and scooped her into his arms. He had her in the middle of the bed and his body atop hers before she could react. His mouth covered one of her breasts, his tongue flicking across her nipple until she whimpered. Moving to the other side, he murmured something about how gorgeous she was before doing the same with her other breast.

Needing something to hold onto, Emma twined her fingers into his dark hair, her fingernails scraping his scalp. She felt him shiver, heard his labored breathing, and thrilled when his good hand smoothed down her belly, through her damp curls, and to her thighs. Knowing some of what to do, she parted her knees in invitation and almost drew them shut when his fingers slid past her folds and circled her most private place.

"Did I hurt you?" He stilled his fingers.

"Startled me, is all. Do continue. Please."

He chuckled softly, reveling in how she angled her hips to welcome his touch. When he heard her breaths shorten and her soft whimpers increase in volume, he quickened his ministrations until he heard his name called out and her body quivered. He ceased moving his hand when one of hers suddenly covered it.

His need for her too great, he

didn't give her time to catch her breath. He hooked his arms beneath her knees to lift them and then drove his manhood into her in one hard thrust.

Emma's back arched in response, and he seemed to drive deeper into her before he pulled nearly all the way out of her.

He might have paused to prevent what he feared was about to happen, but his body required surcease. He had been too close to his release the moment before he lifted her onto the bed. Now that her thighs gripped his and her fingernails were probably leaving half-moon indentations in his back, Robert knew she was his. Only a few more thrusts, and his entire body spasmed, the intense pleasure blinding him to everything but the soft body beneath him.

Managing to hold himself up on his outstretched arms for only a few seconds, he dipped his head down and kissed Emma. Then he collapsed atop her, his head ending face down in the pillow next to hers.

"Are you all right?"

He chuckled and eventually lifted himself onto his elbows. Glancing down, he saw how her breasts were mounded against his chest. "You are gorgeous." He was about to roll off of her when she tightened her grip on his back.

"Where are you going?"

He dropped his head to her shoulder. "Next to you, if that's all right."

"You're still... inside me," she murmured.

Grinning, he nodded. "Trust me when I tell you it's heaven."

"Then don't go."

Robert kissed her on the lips. "Hang onto me."

"I thought I..." Emma let out a shriek when he suddenly rolled onto his back, taking her body with him. She ended up atop him so close to the edge, one of her knees couldn't gain purchase. Sure he was about to pass out, Robert managed to center himself on the bed and pulled her head down to his shoulder.

"How is that?" His voice seemed to fading. "Are you comfortable?"

"You seem entirely too pleased with yourself."

"Oh, I am," he admitted. He kissed the top of her head. "You should be, too."

Emma gave a start, heartened at hearing his assessment. "Do you suppose we can do it again?" Despite how long it had been since he had pleasured her with his hand, tingles still darted through her, and awareness had her feeling all buzzy.

She felt more than heard his chuckle beneath her body followed by an incoherent mumble and something about two more times before morning and every day after they were married.

"Married?" she repeated. She was about to protest when she sensed they weren't alone.

"*Meow*."

"*Meow.*"

"According to the cats we're going to be."

Emma tittered and reached down to capture the edge of the blanket. She pulled it over them before settling her head into the small of his shoulder.

She fell asleep with a grin on her face as General and Admiral joined them on the bed, their purrs sending the most pleasant vibrations through the bed.

Perhaps marriage wouldn't be so bad after all.

AUTHOR NOTES

Why are biscuits called cookies in the United States?

The original term "biscuit" derives from the Latin "bis coctus," or "twice baked." The rations of Ancient Roman armies included biscuits. Hard tack, ship's biscuits, rusk, Mandelbrot, and zweiback all descend from this culinary lineage. With advances in technology came a wider range of biscuit products. Small cakes and delicate wafers were gradually added to the family of biscuits.

In most English-speaking countries, the traditional definition of biscuit remains. In the United States the term "biscuit" meant a small, soft, quick-leavened bread served hot with a meal.

In England, it came to mean a kind of crisp dry bread more or less hard, prepared generally in thin flat cakes.

In the US, "cookie" was introduced to the English language during the 18th century via the Dutch. While the English primarily referred to cookies as small cakes, seed biscuits, or tea cakes, or by specific names, such as jumbal or macaroon, the Dutch called them koekjes, a diminutive of koek (cake). With the revolutionary tradition of separating the US from all things British, the Dutch heritage prevailed.

Your Invitation!

Do you crave historical romance filled with passion and red hot chemistry?

Come join me and my author friends in the Facebook group, Historical Harlots, for exclusive giveaways, chats with amazing HistRom authors, raunchy shenanigans, and more! https://www.facebook.com/groups/ 2102138599813601

ABOUT THE AUTHOR

A self-described nerd and lover of science, Linda Rae spent many years as a published technical writer specializing in 3D graphics workstations, software and 3D animation (her movie credits include SHREK and SHREK 2). Mythology, immortality, and ancient Greece have been lifelong interests.

A fan of action-adventure movies, she can frequently be found at the local cinema. Although she no longer has any tropical fish, she does follow the San Jose Sharks. She makes her home in Cody, Wyoming.

For more information:
www.lindaraesande.com
Sign up for Linda Rae's newsletter:
Regency Romance with a Twist

For articles on research and travels,
read Linda's Rae blog:
Regency Romance with a Twist